Blondie McGhee
At Your Service

Written by Ashley Eneriz
Illustrated by Catherine Villanueva

Table of Contents

Special Offer for a Free Audiobook

Thank you so much for your purchase of Blondie McGhee: At Your Service!

Please enjoy your free audiobook version of this book.

Just go to:
http://bit.ly/1TYK37E

Chapter One

Detective for Hire

Got a crime?

Need a professional detective?

You've come to the right girl. Kids at Graham Elementary know me as Blondie, the secret detective. Though, I guess it isn't much of a secret if that is what I'm known for.

Despite popular belief, I am not called Blondie just because my hair is blonde, but because my parents had a moment of insanity when I was born. They named me Blondelle after a great- great, French grandmother or something like that.

Have you ever met a Blondelle? Me neither. Once I upgrade my super detective kit, I hope to find all the Blondelles in the world to start a club. That is, if I can find one. But I guess my name is not that horrible since everyone just calls me Blondie. Everyone except Owen who calls me "Blonderella" and "Blondzilla." Don't let his dreamy blue eyes fool ya – he's a real meanie. I would never, ever in a thousand years solve a crime for him.

So, you may be wondering how long I've been a pro-detective. Well, it all started last year in Mrs. Jones' third grade class. My grandma, Grams, had just bought me a really nice detective kit with all the works for my birthday. This thing had a

SLOW-POKE

magnifying glass, notebook, gloves, dusting powder, and everything else a real-life detective would need. I got to put it to use when Slow Poke, the third-grade class turtle, went missing. Ever since then, kids have been asking me to solve their mysteries.

THINGS GRAMS LOSES

Now that I am starting fourth grade, I expect business to grow rapidly. I assume more mysteries happen the older you get. I'll prove it. Grams is really old, and she has a new mystery every time I see her.

I have lost count of how many times I've had to find her keys, glasses, and even her teeth – gross! I don't mind so much since she is my only paying customer. She gives me a quarter for each case I solve.

I almost forgot to tell you about my trusty and reliable sidekick, Emma. I would not be the expert I am today without her. Emma is the family dachshund. Dachshund is just a big,

fancy word for weenie dog. In fact, you can call dachshunds

"weenie dogs," "doxies," or "hot dogs." Just don't call them "hot

dogs" on the night your mom serves hot dogs for dinner. They

might get confused.

Emma is the best detective dog ever. It's true that she has never solved a case, but she is really cute and smart and loves to cuddle. I know with more training she really will be the best detective dog around.

"Blondie, are you ready for school?" my mother calls down the hall.

"Yeah, I'm coming," I call back.

I look at Emma sleeping on my lap. I might be the only kid on the planet excited to start school again. Summer is just too hot and boring. Mysteries don't like to happen during summer vacation, unless you count the time Grams couldn't find the jello casserole she made (after grueling hours of detective work, I discovered Emma was the culprit). I did use the summer to brush up on my skills by reading Nancy Drew and by watching old *Murder, She Wrote* episodes with Grams.

I pull Emma off my lap and give her a kiss. "You be good today," I tell her. "You should practice your sniffing skills in the backyard. You still haven't found that doggie treat I hid last week." I pack my detective notebook in my backpack and walk outside towards the car. My older sister has taken the front seat, even though according to the chart I made, it is my turn. I am too excited about school to make a fuss about it. Although, I will be taping a copy of the chart to her door when I get home, just to make sure she gets the message.

As we pull up to Graham Elementary, I brace myself. I just know I am going to be bombarded with kids wanting me to solve their mystery cases. I will simply organize the cases from most important to least, and solve them in that order.

Yes, that will be perfect.

This is going to be the best year yet!

Chapter Two

First Case of the Year

The first week of school has come and gone, and not a single person has asked me to solve a case.

I know the problem! I think in the middle of a very boring math lesson. I have not done enough advertising. I will change that during lunch today.

After the fourth and fifth graders sit down for lunch, I stand up and clear my throat as loudly as I can.

"Excuse me," I call.

No one even glances at me. All the kids are too busy talking and eating their lunches. I climb onto the metal table and stomp my feet a few times. The noise ricochets throughout the cafeteria.

"Excuse me. Everyone look at me!" I shout louder.

There is only silence, and all the kids look at me curiously.

"I just want to remind everyone that I am a detective, and I would be happy to take on any case you might have. No case is too big or too..."

"Blondelle McGhee, get off the table right now," the lunch aide shouts.

"Right. Yes, sorry," I say.

I step down and continue my speech.

"Like I was saying. I will sit here every day for lunch. So feel free to contact me."

It is no use. Everyone goes back to talking, giggling, and taking bites of their food. I sit back down and look at my detective notebook longingly. *I just want one case*, I plead to myself.

"Hiya, Blondie," a voice says behind me.

I turn around excitedly. It is Owen. Behind him, his friends snigger at each other.

"Go away, Owen."

"No, please. I need your help." He sits down next to me. "I have a case," he whispers.

"Sorry, Owen. My services are only available to everyone not named Owen Thomas."

"Please, will you just listen to my case?" he asks.

OWEN THE MEANIE

I sigh but nod my head. I want to solve a case so badly that I will do anything. Even if it means having to work with Owen.

"Okay, great. But you need to keep it on the down-low. It is a little embarrassing."

I flip open my detective notebook and touch the sharp pencil tip to my tongue. I'm not sure what this does, but I've seen several detectives and cops do it on TV.

"Give me the deets," I say.

"The what?" Owen asks.

I sigh loudly. "The details."

"Right," he says and looks back at his two friends, Matt and Mike, as they nudge each other and laugh.

"I'll catch up with you guys later," Owen says to his friends. They both walk away laughing. I will never quite understand the mystery of boys.

"The other day when Mrs. Clemmons asked me to take something to the office, I heard a scary noise coming from the janitor's closet," Owen starts. "I didn't think anything of it until I heard the same, exact scary noise at the same time the next day when I went to the bathroom. I knocked on the door, and the noise grew even louder. Then I heard the doorknob turn, so I hid behind the water fountain."

"What happened next," I ask, engrossed in the story.

"Aren't you going to write any of this down?" he asks.

I look down at my blank notebook. "Yes. Scary noises, heard two times," I say as I jot it down. "What time did you hear these noises?"

"1:45," Owen answers.

"That is during quiet reading time," I say aloud to myself. "So what happened after you heard the doorknob turn?"

"Well, then the janitor lady came out."

"Miss Carrie," I correct him.

"Yes, Miss Carrie, but when she came out, she had fangs."

"Fangs!" I yell in disbelief.

"Shhh! Keep it down. Will ya?" he says looking behind him to make sure no one is listening.

"Sorry," I whisper back. "But come on. Fangs?"

"Look. I am just telling you what I saw," he said waving his hands defensively.

"Okay. I will start investigating today."

"Are you actually going to go in there?" he asks.

"Well, I suppose I have to."

As Owen walks away, I think about my plan. Since I already finished two chapter books during reading time last week, Mrs. Clemmons will probably let me leave the classroom. But the real question is, how am I going to be gone from the classroom for twenty minutes without raising suspicion?

Aha! Owen.

QQQ

"Mrs. Clemmons," I say after the rest of the class settles down for quiet reading time. "I am not feeling the best. May I use the restroom?"

"Of course! If you need to get some crackers or ginger ale from the office, too, go right ahead."

Mrs. Clemmons is one of the nicest teachers I have ever had. I feel a little guilty that I am devising this plan behind her back. Though, I guess I am not technically lying to her. My stomach does feel a little funny, but that is probably because I didn't have any time to eat my lunch between the announcement I made and listening to Owen tell me about his case.

Right after the lunch bell rang, I told Owen to wait five minutes after I left to go up to Mrs. Clemmons' desk. He is supposed to ask for homework help to keep Mrs. Clemmons distracted. Owen can hardly be considered a good student, so Mrs. Clemmons should definitely buy his act. Now that I think of it, a little extra homework help might do Owen some good. Good detectives always figure out how to solve multiple problems with one solution.

I walk slowly to the girl's bathroom and check my surroundings. The hallway is clear, and I spot the janitor's closet a few feet before the bathroom. A partial, white, powdery footprint is in front of the door.

That's weird, I think.

I bend down and swipe the powder with my finger. The powder is fine but does not have a strong odor. I rub my fingers together. It reminds me of the time I made sugar cookies with Grams, and I had to cover my hands in flour to keep the cookies from being sticky.

I pull out my notebook and write, "Partial footprint in front of closet. White powder-possibly flour."

Then I hear a rustling sound followed by a noise I don't even know how to explain. All I know is it makes the hairs on the back of my neck stand up.

"Detectives don't get scared," I say quietly. I pull a bobby pin from my hair to pick the lock. I have never actually picked a lock before, but surely it can't be that hard. All the detectives in the movies I watch make it look easy.

As I bend down to the knob, I realize I don't need my bobby pin after all. The door is unlocked. I begin to twist the door knob slowly when I hear the noise again.

I inhale sharply. "I can do this," I whisper. I open the door slightly and look up and down the hall one last time before entering. I peek inside the room, but it is too dark. I slip inside and quickly shut the door behind me.

The room smells strongly of cleaning supplies, so I put my sleeve over my nose and try to block out the smell. I carefully feel around me for objects, but since I cannot see anything, I knock something to the floor with a small clanging noise.

A low growling fills the room. I panic and fall backwards into the door. As fast as I can, I feel up and down the wall until I find the light switch, and light fills the room. My eyes connect with a huge, terrifying eye, and I scream louder than I have ever screamed before.

In front of me is a scary, green monster with one bulging eye. His other eye is missing and so is the skin around his mouth. While I am screaming, a cloud of white dust explodes into the air, and I inhale it in. The white dust falls all over me, making me cough and gag. During all of this confusion, I notice something strange. Those aren't monster hands.

I calm down when I realize that this monster has human hands and legs. This monster is also wearing the same exact outfit that Mike, Owen's best friend, was wearing at lunch.

"Mike," I squeal angrily. "What is the big idea?"

He can't answer me because he is hunched over with his arms around his stomach and laughing hysterically.

Just then, the door knob turns.

Chapter Three

Deceived

Mike stops laughing, and we look up and see Principal Johnson staring down at us. His brown eyes squint in anger.

"What are you both doing in here?"

Before I have a chance to explain, Mike blurts out, "Owen made me do it. It is all his fault."

"Follow me, please," he says sternly.

"Even me, Principal Johnson?" I ask. Surely he must know that I never get in trouble.

"Yes, even you, Blondelle McGhee."

I really hate when grown ups used my full name.

Mike and I follow Principal Johnson down the hall to our classroom. A little bit of white powder falls off of me with each step I take. When we get to the fourth grade room, several kids tap their neighbor and point at me. The class breaks out in hushed excitement as they whisper amongst themselves. I can't hear what they are saying, but I hear my name several times.

"There should be no talking!" Mrs. Clemmons says sharply. She turns her attention to us and her mouth makes an "O" shape when she sees me. I can only imagine what I look like. My face feels dry from the flour, and the corner of my right eye stings a little bit.

"Mrs. Clemmons, I would like to see Owen Thomas, please," Principal Johnson says flatly.

Owen hangs his head as he walks towards us.

"Good going, Blondie. You just had to tell on me, didn't you?"

"Hardly," I say, putting my hand on my hip. "Mike blamed it all on you quicker than you can say detention."

Principal Johnson clears his throat. "I don't want any more talking until we get to my office."

QQQ

Principal Johnson doesn't seem too interested in hearing my side of the story. He says I am still in trouble for wandering around the school when I was not supposed to, even if I was pretending to be a detective. Pretending! Won't anyone take my detective work seriously?

When we are in the principal's office, he tells all three of us that he is going to call our parents and that we all have a strike against us. He looks especially angry at Owen since this is his second strike.

I try not to laugh when Principal Johnson tells Owen that if he gets one more strike he will be expelled. Now that would be a dream come true! Can you imagine school without Owen Thomas? That is what I call a vacation!

I clean myself off the best that I can, which, by the way, is not an easy task. Have you ever tried to get wet flour out of your hair? By the time I am ready to leave the girl's bathroom, the last school bell rings. Thank goodness today is over. Now, I just have to explain the whole situation to my parents and hope they will understand.

"Look, here comes Scaredy Detective!" Owen calls out as I walk to the pick-up line. All of the fourth graders laugh.

"Got a crime? I'll run away screaming," Matt adds and the kids laugh even harder. Before I can retort, my mom pulls up in her white SUV.

"Do you want to explain why Principal Johnson had to call me in the middle of an important meeting today?" My mother's harsh voice fills the car as I climb into

my seat. I open my mouth to answer, but no words escape. Instead, I burst into tears.

My mom looks back at me and must realize I am covered in white dots of flour, because her angry face relaxes a bit.

"Oh sweetheart," she says, but she doesn't say anything else. She just turns towards the windshield and starts driving. I think she might be saving the rest of her anger for when we get home.

But we don't go home. Instead, she drives to my favorite fast food restaurant, Jolly Burgers. When she gets to the speaker, she says, "I will have two banana-nutty sundaes, please."

Those are my favorite. I am afraid to ask if one is for me, because I definitely do not deserve one.

I sit quietly in the backseat waiting until we get home. *Wait a second, this is not the way we take to go home.* I don't dare ask where my mom is taking me. In these types of situations, it is best to be quiet and hope your parents don't remember what you did wrong. Perhaps we will do so many errands she will forget that the principal ever called her.

She pulls into the parking lot of my favorite park. I am too big for the jungle gym, now that I am nine, but I still love sitting under the trees. I usually like to bring Emma so she can chase the squirrels and bark at anything she wants without my mom scolding her. She can chase those squirrels for hours and not even get tired. Man, it must be nice to be a dog. You definitely do not have to deal with any Owens or Principal Johnsons when you have four paws.

My mom parks the car, grabs the sundaes, and says, "Follow me," before I have a chance to ask any questions. She leads me to my favorite bench which just happens to be right by my favorite tree. Something suspicious is going on.

She slides me a sundae and opens her own.

"For me?" I ask.

She throws her head back and laughs. "Of course, silly. I'm not going to eat both of them. Do you want to tell me about today?"

I sigh before I take a bite of ice cream. "I just really wanted to solve a mysterious case," I explain. "I didn't mean to get in trouble or to break any rules."

"I know, honey. Sometimes you have to realize that even though rules are not fun, they are there to keep you safe."

"I definitely understand that now. If I had stayed in class, those annoying boys wouldn't have covered me in flour and made the whole class laugh at me." A tear begins to roll down my cheek. I am trying really hard not to be a cry-baby about it, but it was just so embarrassing!

My mom reaches over and touches my hand, "You want to hear a funny story?"

I grumble. "Is this like the story of when you met Dad? Because if it is, that story was not very funny or interesting, no offense."

She laughs again. "No, this one is a funny story. I promise."

"Okay."

"When I was your age, I wanted to be the most popular girl in my class. I thought that all the girls would think I was cool if I wore these stylish white pants. Of course, it was also the day the cafeteria served spaghetti and meatballs for lunch. I was so focused on watching a guy that I thought was cute, that I sat right on a plate of spaghetti and meatballs! The whole school saw it and laughed, even the cute guy. Then, when I went to the office to call my mom, I was pretty sure I could hear the office ladies laughing too. The worst part was that my mom was helping my grandma that day, so no one could bring me a new pair of pants."

I covered my mouth to keep ice cream from spilling out. I was laughing so hard. "So how did you get over everyone laughing at you?" I ask when I can finally manage to talk again.

"Well, thankfully, your Grandpa Joe got a new work assignment, and we had to move to a different state the next month. I was able to start over at my new school, and I have never worn white pants since."

"So, can we move?" I ask hopefully.

"Nope, but I bet the kids will forget this incident in a month or so."

I grumble again. A month of fourth grade will feel like eternity!

Q

Chapter Four

Food Fight

My mom's talk made me feel better, but I still didn't want to go to school when I woke up.

"I don't feel good," I complain to my mom. I put my hand on my stomach for extra good measure.

My mom tilts her head sideways and smirks.

"You don't feel good?" she asks.

I can tell she doesn't believe me. Moms are born with super detective skills. They can always tell when you are lying or planning on doing something naughty. They don't even need training.

She gave me a smile. "Okay. I'll call Grams, and she can stay with you today."

Staying home from school always seems like a good idea until you turn on the TV. There is never anything good on, only boring, old-people shows. Normally I don't mind watching TV with Grams, but a girl can only take so many *The Price Is Right* reruns.

Every time I look at the clock, I imagine what I would be doing at school if I was there.

8 a.m. - Science: Today, we were going to find out about our science fair. I am a little sad I'm missing school today.

10 a.m. - P.E.: Thank goodness I am missing running practice in P.E. today. They say it stands for physical education, but I am pretty certain is stands for "pure evil." Good thing I skipped school today.

11:00 a.m. - Read-Aloud Hour: Oh, man! I am missing the next part of *The BFG*. Why did I stay home?

12:00 p.m. - Lunch: I'm sure everyone is laughing about what happened yesterday. I am so glad I stayed home!

By the time 2:45 rolls around, my brain feels like jelly

from watching too much TV with Grams. When parents warn

you not to watch too much television, they mean it. Grams is

snoring away in our blue recliner, and Emma is sleeping, too,

curled up next to her. That's the funny thing about grandmas

and dogs. They both take a bazillion

naps every day!

The door bell rings, and I

race to the peephole to see

who it is.

Owen Thomas!

What in the world is he doing

on my front porch?! It is true that he lives

just down the street, but he has never been to my house before.

I open the door slowly and poke out my head.

"What are you doing here, Owen?" I ask meanly.

"Uh, hi, Blondie. I just came over to say, 'I'm sorry for yesterday.'"

"Well, if that is all, I will see you tomorrow," I say, shutting the door.

"Wait!" Owen cries.

I open the door again.

"I need your help."

"I'm not falling for that one again!"

"I'm serious. I really need your help this time," he pleads.

"What? Do you need my help finding the scary monster in your closet, or perhaps you just want to lock me in your basement and throw pudding on me this time?" I am practically yelling at him. But I remember Detective Lesson 53: A detective needs to stay calm in all situations.

Obviously, I am still working on that lesson.

"Will you just listen? Please?"

"Nope. Sorry, Owen, you already had your chance."

He hangs his head low and sits on my porch. He could sit there all night for all I care. I am not going to fall for one of his tricks again. I close the door and see that Grams is standing right behind me.

"Grams! You scared me."

She laughs, which turns into a half-laugh, half-cough, choking sound. "Was that Owen Thomas?"

"Yes. How did you know?"

"I go to bingo with his grandma. He is such a sweet boy!"

"He is everything in the world that is opposite of sweet!" I exclaim.

"What makes you say that?"

"Grams, he played a mean trick on me yesterday, and now he is acting like he did nothing wrong and is asking for my help again."

"Blondelle, I know it is hard to be nice to people who are mean to us, but it is very important that we learn how to forgive them."

"Okay. I forgive him. Want to watch a movie?" I say quickly, trying to change the subject.

Grams does her half-laugh, half-cough noise again.

"Why don't you tell Owen you forgive him, and give him a second chance?"

I sigh loudly. "Fine."

She gives me a wink and walks away.

When I open the door, Owen turns to look at me and wipes quickly at his eyes.

"Are you..."

"No!" he interrupts me quickly.

"Look, don't cry," I start.

"I'm not crying," he grumbles.

"I will help you."

"You will?" His face bursts into a huge smile, and he jumps up and hugs me. It is a good thing I know for a fact that cooties are not real, because if they were, I would be covered in them right now. While cooties might not be a real thing, Owen is definitely covered in icky boy germs, so I try to push him off as quickly and nicely as possible.

"I will help you only under one condition," I add.

"What?" he asks.

"You have to pinky promise me that you will not trick me and that you will tell everyone I am the best detective ever." I hold out my pinky and he locks his pinky with mine.

"Okay. Now, what do you need help with?" I ask, sitting on the porch. There is a spare piece of chalk next to me, and I pick it up and play with it in my fingers. Detective Lesson 111: Even if you don't have your detective notebook handy, you should always be ready to write down important details.

"You mean you haven't heard?"

"Heard what?" I don't know how he expected me to have heard anything. I wasn't at school all day, and I highly doubt he was cool enough to make it onto the news.

"I was expelled today."

"What? How?" I am not sure if I am more confused or relieved.

"Principal Johnson thinks I started the food fight at lunch today." A food fight?! I miss school for one day and the two most exciting things happen: an actual, real-life, food fight, and Owen is expelled. I am never missing school again!

"Well, did you?" I ask.

"No, of course not, but he doesn't exactly believe me since I have already been in trouble several times this year."

"I don't blame him."

"Hey, I thought you were going to help me."

"Relax. I am. So tell me everything that happened. Don't leave out any details."

"Well, after I got my lunch, I sat down next to Mike. We were talking about Minecraft, and the next thing I know, something gross hit me in the face. It surprised me, so I yelled and wiped it off quickly. Then the next thing I know, there was food flying everywhere."

"Why did Principal Johnson think you started the fight?"

"That lame fifth grader, Corey Perkins, said I threw food on him."

"And what kind of food hit you in the face?"

"How am I supposed to know?"

"Do you remember what color it was?"

"Uh, white. I think."

"And was it cold or hot?"

"Definitely warm," he answers.

"So we can safely rule out ice cream," I conclude. I look closer at his face, looking for any leftover food particles.

"Why are you looking at me like that?"

"I'm looking for evidence."

"On my face?" he exclaims.

"Shh! There! Found some," I say, finding a small white glob near his ear. One thing you can count on in life: boys are not the best cleaners. I wipe the glob off his face with my finger.

"Now for the gross part," I whisper. I sniff it. Then, I close my eyes and stick the glob in my mouth. I try to let it linger as long as possible on my tongue, and I try not to think about the fact that this piece of food was sitting on Owen's face all day. Yuck!

"Did you seriously just eat that?" Owen has the most disgusted look on his face.

"Sometimes a detective has to do what a detective has to do," I explain. "And I think the mystery food was mashed potatoes."

"Oh, yeah. When Corey told on me, he said that he was hit with mashed potatoes."

"Thanks a lot," I say. "If you had remembered that part, I wouldn't have had to eat them off your face."

Chapter Five

The Real First Case of the Year

As I enter the courtyard Wednesday morning, I feel a lot of eyes on me. I see kids whispering to each other and pointing at me.

"Here comes the best, I mean, the scarediest detective in the world," Mike calls out.

Matt elbows him and hisses, "Shhh." If the whole fourth and fifth grade classes were not already looking at me, they are now. I beg and plead with my mom to drop me off late, but she just gives me one of those looks. You know, the look that says, "Blondie, you are really pushing it."

"Good morning, everyone," I say loudly. "As you might know, Owen Thomas has been expelled."

The kids gasp and start to whisper excitedly.

"Well, I guess some of you didn't know that. The point is that Owen says he did not start the food fight yesterday, and I am going to get to the bottom of who really did start the food fight. If anyone has any information about yesterday and the real perpetrator, please come find me at the swings during recess."

The start-of-school bell rings just as I finish my speech, and all of the kids flood towards the door. I am not sure if anyone fully heard me or paid attention to what I was saying.

"Uh, hi there, Blondie," Mike says. "Look, I'm sorry about earlier. Thanks for trying to get Owen off the hook for the food fight."

"Mike, just the person I wanted to talk to," I say, pulling out my detective notebook and purple gel pen.

"Where were you during the food fight?" I ask.

He scratches his head and looks a little confused. It is hard to tell if he is thinking or what, because, quite honestly, he always looks confused.

"Oh!" He exclaims. "I remember. I was telling Owen about the new Minecraft character skins that were coming out."

So far, Owen's story is checking out. "Did you see Owen throw any food – be honest?"

"No! I promise. One minute we were talking, and the next minute he was screeching because he had food on his face."

I jot this down quickly. "Thank you for your help."

"No problem. I'll do anything I can to help," he adds.

"Actually, there is one more thing. I need to talk to Corey Perkins at lunch time. Can you help me with that?"

"I'll try my best," Mike answers. "But that guy is kind of scary."

By the time recess comes around, I already have made a list of suspects and people I want to question. I bring my detective notebook and pen with me, just in case. The swings are empty when I get there, and I am afraid that no one will come forward with information.

I shouldn't have worried. Fourth grader, James Little, sits on the swing next to me.

"I think I have some information," he says.

"Name?" I ask, whipping out my pen.

"You already know my name," he answers.

"James, you have to follow proper protocol. Now, name please."

"James Little."

"Thank you. Now, James, tell me in your own words what happened Tuesday."

"Well, I was eating my peanut butter and jelly sandwich, and then I heard yelling. Corey Perkins yelled something at his friend, and then, he threw his pudding cup on him."

"What about Owen?"

"I never saw Owen do anything."

"What happened after Corey threw his pudding on his friend?"

"All I remember was a lot of pushing and shoving at the fifth grade tables, and then food started flying all over the place."

"Anything else?"

James shakes his head. "Just don't tell anyone that I told you, okay?"

I nod and look up. A small line has formed in front of my swing.

"Next," I call.

A fifth grade girl sits next to me.

"Name?" I ask, looking down at my notebook.

"Shawna," she says quietly.

"Okay, Shawna. Please tell me what you saw yesterday."

"Um, I'm not sure, but I think I saw a bunch of fourth grade girls smashing pizza into each others faces."

"Pizza?" I ask.

"Yeah or something like that. Corey had nothing to do with the food fight. It was all the fourth grader's fault."

"Thank you for your information, Shawna. Next!" I call.

A third grade boy stands in front of me.

"Can I help you?" I ask, slightly annoyed.

"I was just waiting for my turn on the swing," he says timidly.

"Sorry, I am conducting official detective work. There will be no swinging today."

He grumbles and walks away. Sometimes it can be a pain sharing recess with the younger kids.

"Next," I call.

Another fifth grade girl sits next to me on the swing.

"Name?" I ask.

"Ava," she says and snaps her bubble gum. We aren't allowed to have gum at school, but obviously Ava is a rule-breaker. I write that part down in really tiny letters so she can't see what I'm writing.

"Alright, Ava. Tell me what happened yesterday."

"Owen totally started the food fight," she exclaims.

"Oh really?" I am a little surprised by how confident she is in her answer.

"He threw hot soup on Corey Perkins because Corey was talking to a girl he liked."

"What?" I exclaim.

"Yeah, and I heard that his parents are sending him to an all-boy army boot camp or something."

"You do realize your story does not match anyone else's, right?"

"Look, I'm just telling you what I heard," she says, getting off the swing.

"And where, exactly, did you hear this from, if you don't mind me asking?"

The bell rings. Ava looks at me and snaps her gum again.

"Sorry, if I am late for P.E. one more time, Mrs. Knapp is going to make me wear the ugly uniform," she says before running off.

The ugly P.E. uniform is one I know about all too well. It has a disgusting stain on the front and smells like mildew. At the beginning of the year, I had to wear it for an entire week all because the office ordered my P.E. uniform two sizes too big. I still can't figure out why I had to suffer for a clerical error.

Chapter Six

Stick a Fork in Me

When I walk into the cafeteria for lunch, I walk as slowly

as possible. I want to take in every little detail. I am trying to

imagine what happened the day before. I don't want to miss

even the smallest of clues.

"Blondie, are you okay?" Matt asks.

"Yes, why?"

"Because you are moving slower than my grandpa, and

he is like, 100," he laughs.

My mind is too focused on the case to laugh or come up

with a witty retort, so I just get straight to the point. "Where

were you and Owen sitting yesterday?"

"Where we always sit. The second table." He points

towards the second blue table on the right side of the cafeteria.

"Doesn't Owen usually sit next to the wall, though?" I ask, trying to piece the scene together.

"Yes, but yesterday Mrs. Clemmons made two girls sit at our table, so Owen had to sit on the very edge. There was barely enough room for him."

"Then that means Corey must have been sitting...right here," I say, walking to the spot. My guess is correct, because a very large, fifth grade boy, who I suspect is Corey, is sitting in that same spot now.

"Did someone say my name?" Corey asks.

"Good luck with that," Matt says, walking away.

I take a deep breath. To say that Corey Perkins is a little intimidating is an understatement.

"Yes, I did," I answer him, trying to sound as brave as I can.

"And who are you?" He asks as he takes a large bite of his sandwich.

"Blondie McGhee," I say and stick out my hand.

He looks at it and then looks at his friends. They all laugh. I guess hand shakes are too formal for most elementary school kids, or perhaps Corey hasn't been told that cooties are not real. I sit down across from him.

"Hey," another boy yells. "Fourth graders aren't allowed to sit on this side of the cafeteria."

I clear my throat. "I will only be a minute. I need to ask Corey a few questions."

"Ooh, Corey. Is that your secret crush?" the boy teases.

"Enough Dean, or I'll tell everyone what's hiding in your desk. Ribbit, ribbit."

Dean's eyes bulge. He quickly shuts his mouth and slumps back into his seat.

"Look," Corey says, turning his attention towards me. "I don't want to spend all my lunch hour talking to a fourth grader."

"Just give me five minutes, and I will be out of your hair," I promise.

He grunts, which I take to mean "yes" in fifth grade boy language.

"What happened yesterday at lunch?" I ask.

"That Owen kid threw mashed potatoes at me for no reason. That's what happened."

"I heard that you yelled at your friends and threw a pudding cup on one of them"

"Who told you that?"

"I am not at liberty to say, but if you could tell me your side of the story, then I won't mention the pudding cup to Principal Johnson."

"Fine," he grumbles.

"Like I said, that Owen kid threw mashed potatoes on my shirt. All of my friends started laughing at me. I don't like to be laughed at, so I yelled at them to stop. Most of them did, except Todd. He kept laughing and yelling that a bird pooped on me, so I threw my pudding in his face."

I clamp my lips together to keep from laughing.

"Then what happened?"

"Then Todd pushed me and tried to throw pudding on me, but he missed and hit Lydia and George instead. Then everyone started throwing food."

"Do you really think Owen started the food fight though?"

"I think your five minutes are up. Beat it."

I sigh. Fifth graders can be so mean sometimes.

As I stand up, something shiny by the trashcan catches my eye. *What is that?* I walk over to inspect it.

It is a silver fork. A real fork. What mom would actually trust their kid to take a real fork to school and bring it back? My mom made that mistake once, and boy was she mad when she found out that I accidentally threw the fork away. From that day forward, it was only plastic forks for me.

I take a closer look at the fork. It has white globs of food on it. This has to be the crime weapon!

Thankfully, I keep extra evidence bags, a.k.a sandwich bags, in my lunch box, at all times.

When collecting evidence, make sure you do not touch it. It is very important not to get your fingerprints on the evidence, or you might end up being blamed for the crime. I place my hand in one sandwich bag, carefully pick up the fork, and place it in another sandwich bag.

QQQ

Even though I've found a crucial piece of evidence, I still feel so far away from solving the case. Owen is waiting for me on the porch when I get home.

"So, how did it go? Did you find out who really started the food fight?" his face looks hopeful.

"I'm sorry, Owen. I didn't find out a lot of information today."

"Oh."

He sits on the porch and puts his head in his hands.

"Don't give up yet, Owen. It was only the first day."

"What if you don't find anything?" he asks.

"I'll keep looking. I'll find out what really happened."

"Well, I start my new school on Monday, so maybe it's pointless after all." He stands up and starts to walk away.

"Don't say that, Owen."

"See you around, I guess," he says solemnly. "Tell Matt and Mike I say, 'Hi.'"

I watch him walk down the driveway, towards his house.

Sometimes after a long day at work, my dad comes home and says, "Stick a fork in me, I'm done." It always makes me laugh, but I never really understood why he said it, until today. I spent all day interviewing people and looking for clues, and I am just done! Go ahead and stick a fork in me, just not the fork with mashed potatoes on it. I still need that for evidence.

Chapter Seven

Taco Tuesday

It is Thursday morning, and I am sitting at my desk with my head in my hands. Yesterday's leads were useless, and I am still not fully over the embarrassment of Monday afternoon's disaster. I am even ninety-five percent positive that I heard someone cough, "Scaredy Detective" when I walked in this morning.

Mrs. Clemmons stands before the class and smiles. "Before we start our lesson, let me pass out some paperwork for next week."

Mrs. Clemmons passes out bright orange papers to the class that read, "October's Lunch Menu." As the paper hits my desk, my eyes fall on the Tuesday column. *I've got it!*

"Taco Tuesday!" I shout excitedly and pump my fist in the air.

The class turns and giggles.

"Yes, Blondie," Mrs. Clemmons says seriously. "Every Tuesday has been, and will be, Taco Tuesday. Please refrain from shouting out again."

I nod but can barely hear what she says next. The connections are being made in my head, and I have a hard time concentrating on the math lesson.

When the bell rings for recess, I race to find Matt and Mike. I'm out of breath by the time I reach them on the basketball court. I wave my hands frantically to get their attention.

They look at each other and then, look back at me oddly.

"What did you guys eat for lunch on Tuesday?" I ask, panting.

"Tacos," they say together with smirks on their faces. Mike adds a "duh" right after, and they both laugh.

"What about Owen? Did he get a hot lunch or did he bring a packed lunch?"

"He always gets hot lunch," Matthew answers.

"Yes!" I shout and jump into the air. I am too excited to stay still.

"I don't get it. What's the big deal?" Mike asks.

I can't answer him because I'm already running to Mrs. Clemmons to ask if I can go to the cafeteria to say I can't remember if I ordered hot lunch today or not. I know I didn't, and I hate to lie again, but I am so close to closing this case!

$$QQQ$$

I peek into the cafeteria kitchen and see Mrs. Evans putting little brown square pieces on a big silver tray.

"Hi, Mrs. Evans. Do you mind if I ask you a few questions?"

"What are you doing in here?" she asks, looking slightly annoyed.

"Mrs. Clemmons gave me permission."

"Alright, but I don't have a lot of time to be answering questions. Lunch is an hour away, and I have to make two hundred pizza pockets, a pot of macaroni and cheese, and steamed broccoli before then."

"I'll help," I say, cheerfully.

She slides over a box of gloves. They are too big for my hands, but I don't complain. I am not even sure if kids are supposed to help in the cafeteria, but I don't mention that part either. I just copy the way she arranges the frozen pizza pockets on the silver trays.

Detective Lesson 152: Sometimes if you want answers,

you have to do the grunt work.

"Do you know Owen Thomas?" I ask.

She pauses and thinks. "Oh, yes. He's such a sweet boy."

Why does everyone keep saying that?

"Does he get hot lunch every day?"

"Yes, except yesterday. I did not see him. Why do you ask?"

"Owen has been expelled," I say nonchalantly.

"What?" she exclaims loudly. She is so startled by this news that she almost drops the tray of pizza pockets. I wonder for a split second if she would still serve them for lunch if she had dropped them. Remind me never to order hot lunch again!

"Yes, Principal Johnson thinks he started the food fight on Tuesday."

"Impossible! Owen is such a good boy."

I try to refrain from laughing. She obviously has spent too many hours in front of the microwave.

"What did you serve for lunch on Tuesday?" I ask.

"Tacos," she says. "We always serve tacos on Tuesday."

Even though I know the answer, it is always important to verify.

"Well, the food fight was started by someone who was eating mashed potatoes. Do you know of any students who bring mashed potatoes to school?"

She laughs. "Kids don't bring those kinds of lunches. They bring sandwiches and those weird looking packages with crackers and cheese but definitely not mashed potatoes."

"Can you think of anyone who would bring mashed potatoes to school?"

"No, sorry," she says. The recess bell rings, and I slide off my gloves.

"Thanks for all your help," I say as I leave. Truthfully, she wasn't very helpful at all.

"Wait a second," she says before I leave. "Now that I think of it...Mr. Riley is always in here heating up his lunch. I would ask him or another teacher if they ever bring mashed potatoes for lunch."

I run up and hug her.

"Thank you!" I exclaim. This just might be the breakthrough I have been looking for.

Mrs. Evans looks confused and thrown off balance, but I have no time to explain the importance of what she just told me. I have to get back to class and work out a few details in my detective notebook.

Chapter Eight

The Proof's in the Mashed Potatoes

The clock ticks extra slow as I wait for the lunch bell to ring.

Tick. Tick. Tick.

Every time I look at the clock, the hand has barley moved.

Finally, a shrill "brrring" fills the air, and my heart races.

I'm out of my seat faster than anyone else. I grab my lunch box and quickly walk to the cafeteria. I want to make sure I get Mr. Riley's attention.

All of the tables are empty in the cafeteria. I spot Mr. Riley's usual spot, and I sit there. It would be productive for me to eat my lunch while I wait, but all I can do is twiddle my thumbs. I am so close to solving this case. I can feel it.

Hurry up, Mr. Riley! Hurry up! I scream inside.

After the fourth and fifth graders come into the cafeteria, I keep my eyes peeled for the redheaded man with the bushy mustache. Finally, Mr. Riley comes out with his Tupperware container of food.

He looks a little confused when he sees me sitting at his table, but I just wave to him anyways.

"Hi, Mr. Riley," I say. "I was wondering if I could ask you a few quick questions."

"OK. I don't see any harm in that." He gives an awkward chuckle and sits down. The other kids might make fun of Mr. Riley's silly disposition, but I think he's a really nice teacher.

"First off," I say. "Would you mind telling me what you had for lunch on Tuesday?"

"Tuesday?" He says thoughtfully while wiping soup from his red mustache. "Well, my wife almost always makes my favorite dinner, meatloaf, on Mondays. So usually, I have leftover meatloaf for lunch on Tuesdays."

"Just meatloaf?"

"With mashed potatoes and green beans. And, if I'm really lucky, a brownie."

I jot this down in my notebook. If I have learned one thing as a detective, it is to never rely on your memory. Always write things down, especially important pieces of evidence, like who ate mashed potatoes on the day of a food fight. This is Detective Lesson 105, or maybe 210, I can't remember.

I open my lunch box and pull out the plastic bag with the silver fork in it.

"Next question. Is this your fork?"

"Oh, my. So that's where my fork went. Mrs. Riley was not too happy when I didn't come home with a fork on Tuesday. Where did you find it?"

"By the trashcan," I say, turning and pointing to the big black can next to the cafeteria doors.

"Why in the world would it be there?" he asks.

"That is exactly what I was going to ask you next."

His face lights up as if he has remembered an important detail.

"I completely forgot. As I was coming out of the kitchen to find my seat, I tripped while trying to take a bite of mashed potatoes." He scratches his head and laughs again.

"Then what happened?"

"I ended up spilling the rest of my lunch all over my sweater. So I went back to my classroom to clean myself up. Thankfully, I always keep an extra pair of clothes here, just in case."

While it is strange that Mr. Riley keeps an extra pair of clothes at school, I refrain from writing it down. *Only the relevant facts*, I tell myself.

"So, if you were in your classroom, then that means you weren't here for the food fight, correct?" I continue my line of questioning.

He shakes his head. "I heard about it, but I missed the whole thing."

"Mr. Riley will you please meet me in Principal Johnson's office in ten minutes?" I stand up quickly, grab the bag with the fork in it, and dart off to the office. Mr. Riley calls my name, but I don't stop. He will understand when he gets there.

Chapter Nine

The Confession

"I need to speak with Principal Johnson," I say frantically to the school secretary. I have to admit that I'm being a bit rude barging into the office, especially since she is talking with a parent.

"Please take a seat, and wait your turn," she says in a sweet voice.

"But it's an emergency," I say.

Principal Johnson opens his door and looks out.

"What's the emergency?" he asks, looking concerned.

"Owen didn't start the food fight," I exclaim.

Principal Johnson exhales loudly, and his worried face quickly turns to an annoyed face.

"Oh, Blondelle. I appreciate you trying to be a good friend, but it is too late for Mr. Thomas now. He will fit in better at a different school."

"But I have proof and a confession. Please just listen to my story, Principal Johnson."

He ushers me into his office and says, "Okay. Please make your story quick."

I pull out my notebook and figure out where to start. Maybe I should have planned what I was going to say first.

"Are you going to tell me?" Principal Johnson asks.

"Yes. It all started when I realized that Owen was hit in the face with mashed potatoes. Then, I found out that fifth grader, Corey Perkins, was hit in the face with the same mashed potatoes after Owen wiped them off his face."

He nods.

"The thing is, the food fight happened on Tuesday. Taco Tuesday." I say, putting extra emphasis on the word "taco."

I wait for Principal Johnson to make the connection on his own, but he doesn't.

"And what is your point, Blondelle?"

"Owen gets hot lunch every day, which means he ate tacos on the day of the food fight, not mashed potatoes."

"I see," Principal Johnson says, rubbing his chin.

"Mr. Riley, on the other hand, did eat mashed potatoes."

"Are you trying to tell me that Mr. Riley started a food fight?" he asks, looking displeased again.

I wave my hands defensively. "He didn't do it on purpose. I checked with Mr. Riley just now, and he told me that he tripped that day and spilled food all over his clothes. Then he said he went back to his classroom to change. However, what he did not realize was that, when he tripped, his fork went flying and so did a huge glob of mashed potatoes. I even found the fork yesterday, and it contains mashed potato particles on it to confirm my theory." I hold up the fork in the bag as proof.

"Blondelle McGhee," a voice booms loudly behind me. It is Mr. Riley, and he does not look like his usual, chipper self.

"Mr. Riley, is it true that you started the food fight on Tuesday?" Principal Johnson asks.

"What? What are you talking about?"

"The mashed potatoes!" I shout. "When you tripped, you accidentally flung them on Owen. Then, when Owen wiped his face off, he accidentally flung them on Corey, and the rest is food fight history at Graham Elementary."

"Oh, my," Mr. Riley says. "I guess I did start the food fight. I am so sorry."

Principal Johnson clears his throat.

"Mr. Riley, I am afraid I am going to have to call your parents and expel you."

"But it was an accident," I cry.

Principal Johnson and Mr. Riley burst out in laughter.

"That was a joke, Blondie. But I will be calling Owen's parents right now to apologize and ask him if he would like to come back to Graham."

Q

Chapter Ten

Owen Pays Up

"Another case solved, Emma," I say while throwing her a tennis ball in the front yard. Emma drops her ball in my lap and then turns her attention to the end of the driveway. She barks excitedly and runs to a boy in a hoodie.

It's Owen.

"Hey, Blondie," he says looking down at his shoes.

"Hey," I reply back.

"Um, look. I just wanted to say thanks. Thanks for everything." His blue eyes lock with mine and my heart flutters a tiny bit. *Ugh! Why do those blue eyes always get me? It's not like I like him or anything!*

"Don't mention it. You didn't deserve to get blamed for something you didn't do," I say.

I don't bother mentioning his pinky promise from earlier. I have a feeling he is going to start being a lot nicer to me from now on. He might even stop calling me "Blondzilla" now that I cleared his name of the food fight.

"Well, I guess I'll see you at school tomorrow," he says, bending down to give Emma a pat on the head.

"Yep, I'll be there waiting for my next mystery to solve."

"And don't worry, I didn't forget about the promise," he grins.

"Alright, class. It is time to settle down," Mrs. Clemmons says on Friday morning. "I've got a surprise for you."

At the word, "surprise," the class falls dead silent. Mrs. Clemmons looks towards the door and waves in Principal Johnson and Owen.

"Owen!" several kids shout out.

"Class, I have something important to tell you," Principal Johnson says when he reaches the front of the classroom.

"I expelled Owen because I thought he started the food fight on Tuesday. It has come to my attention that he did not start the food fight. In fact, the whole situation was just a silly misunderstanding. I have already apologized to Owen, and he is excited to get back to studying...what are you studying?" his voice breaks off as he looks at the chalkboard behind him.

"Ah, the Gold Rush."

Owen beams, and Principal Johnson gives him a pat on the back. "Alright then, I will let Mrs. Clemmons get back to her day."

Owen gives me a wink and then says, "Mrs. Clemmons, may I please make a short announcement?"

Mrs. Clemmons looks taken aback. I wonder if she is surprised that Owen Thomas, for once in his life, has asked a question in the proper way.

"Yes, go ahead, Owen."

"I just want to give a big shout out to Blondzilla over there. She is the best, smartest, and maybe even the cutest detective ever!"

My cheeks feel extremely hot, and I can only imagine what shade of red my face is turning. The class breaks out in "oohs" and "awws" over the fact that Owen just called me cute, but the only word I can focus on is, "Blondzilla."

I sigh.

Some things never change.

Blondie McGhee Training Ahead

Fun Detective Experiments to Try

GROCERY LIST

MANGOES
EGGS
EGGPLANT
TOMATOES
MILK
EGGNOG
BLUEBERRIES
YOGURT
SUGAR
WATERMELON
ICE CREAM
NECTARINES
GRAPES
SALT

How to Send Secret Messages

So you want to be a detective just like me? Great! This world needs as many detectives as possible. Many times when you are solving a case, you will need to write down a secret piece of evidence or give someone a secret message. Or sometimes you want to give your best friend a message without nosy people like Owen Thomas reading it. Here is the easiest way to write secret messages.

1. Write your super secret message on a white piece of paper with a white crayon. You want to make sure to use medium to firm pressure, but don't break the crayon!
2. Give the message to your friend and tell them to paint over it with watercolors.
3. It doesn't matter what color watercolor paint you choose (besides white, of course). After your friend paints the whole page, your secret message will be easy to read.

Sometimes you need to get a secret message to a friend quickly and don't have time to paint with watercolors. Use my grocery list method. For example, if I wanted to tell someone:

Meet me by swings.

I would simply write out the message vertically and then make my message look like a grocery list. Just like this:

Grocery List

Mangoes
eggs
eggplant
tomatoes
Milk
eggnog
Blueberries
yogurt
Sugar
watermelon
ice cream
nectarines
grapes
salt

Just don't make your message too long, and it is best to avoid secret messages with Us, Xs, and Zs since I can't think of any foods that start with those letters!

How to Collect Fingerprints

Some cases will require you to collect fingerprints. For example, if Mr. Riley had denied that the fork was his, I could then get his fingerprints and see if they matched the fingerprints on the fork.

Whether you want to collect fingerprints to solve a crime or just for fun, here is an easy way to do it.

You will need a lead pencil, tape, index card, and a piece of paper.

1. Hold the pencil at an angle on paper and color a small area with the pencil. You will have to color a little harder than normal.
2. Roll the tip of one finger over the pencil coloring.
3. Your piece of tape should sit on the table, sticky side up. Carefully roll your finger on the tape, so that the prints transfer over. You might need someone else's help to get the best print.
4. Then place your piece of tape on an index card. Repeat for each finger and your thumb.
5. Collect fingerprints from your friends and family members too, and compare them with yours. Do you see any similarities or differences?